CHEETAH

CHEETAH

CHEETAH

CHEETAH

CHEETAH

CHEETAH

CHEETAH

CHEETAH

CHEETAH

CHEETAH

For my wife, Colleen.
I totally tricked her into marrying me.

Balzer + Bray is an imprint of HarperCollins Publishers.

Cheetah Can't Lose

Copyright © 2013 by Bob Shea

All rights reserved. Manufactured in China.

Library of Congress Cataloging-in-Publication Data is available.

ISBN 978-0-06-173083-2 (trade bdg.)

Typography by Colleen Shea, Perfectly Nice

12 13 14 15 16   SCP   10 9 8 7 6 5 4 3 2 1

❖

First Edition

Cheetah Can't Lose

BOB SHEA

BALZER + BRAY
An Imprint of HarperCollinsPublishers

Hooray!

It's big race day!

Which big race?

The one I always win because I am big and fast
and you always lose because you are little and cats?

That big race?

Yes, Cheetah.

That big race.

This year will be different!

Let's see. . . . Raise your hand if you are
the fastest animal in the whole wide world.
Hmmm . . . just me, I guess.

That is true, but this year we are having
lots of races so everyone can win!

Or I can win them all! **Let's go!**

First race—
FLOWER JUMPING!

They smell nice.

Pretty!

See? I win!

You are fast, Cheetah!
Your prize is
special winner shoes!
WOW!

Now everyone will know that **I am a champion!**

Maybe we will have better luck in the next race.

A pie-eating race!

GO!

Nom! Nom! Nom!
Nom!
Nom!
Nom! Nom!
Nom!
Nom!
Nom!

One bite!

Two bites!

Five pies!
I win!

WOW!

You win the ice-cream sundae of triumph!

Oh my! I am too full of pie to eat a big sundae.

That is too bad.
The prize now goes to second place!

NO! I am the winner. It is MY sundae!

Oh boy, Cheetah, you have the belly of a true champion.

I don't feel so good.

You are just excited for our next challenge!

YARN POUNCING!

Pounce!

Aw, shucks! We lost again!
Good job, Cheetah!

HA! What has two thumbs
and can't lose?
This guy!

You win victory balloons!
You are very lucky, Cheetah.

It is not luck. It is skill.
I am very skilly.

Last race before the big race!

It is a mind-reading guessing race. I am thinking of a number between three and five. Read my mind to guess the number.

Orange!

**Four!
I win again!**

Oh boy! If you guys had pajamas, I would be them!
Because I'm the cat's pajamas—get it?

Never mind.

Here is your very special and important good-guessing crown!

My head isn't big e̶

Don't be silly. Your head is plenty big!

Now it is time for the most important race of all.
THE BIG RACE!

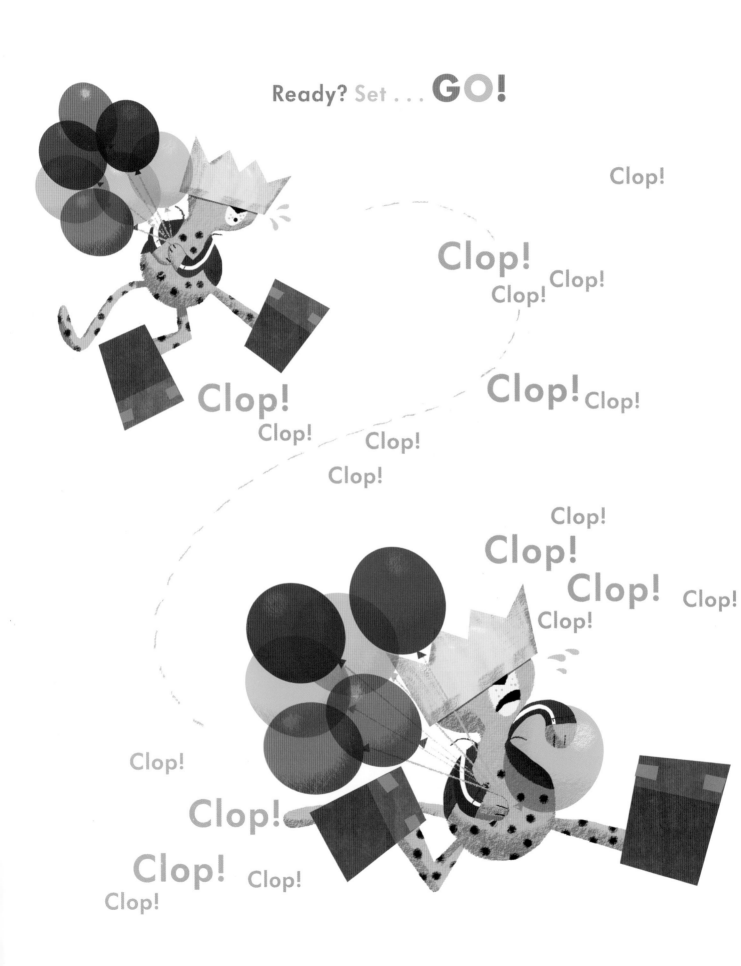

Pop! Pop! Pop! Pop! Pop! Pop! Pop!

CRASH!

HOORAY!!

Are you cheering for me? Did I . . . win?

YES!
You won!

VICTORY!

**You cats are very lucky
to have a friend like me.**

Yes, Cheetah, we really are.

CHEETAH

CHEETAH

CHEETAH

CHEETAH

CHEETAH

CHEETAH

CHEETAH

CHEETAH

CHEETAH